D0996393

This igloo book belongs to:

....

igloobooks

Published in 2014
by Igloo Books Ltd
Cottage Farm
Sywell
NN6 0BJ
www.igloobooks.com

SHE001 0714
2 4 6 8 10 9 7 5 3 1
ISBN 978-1-78343-365-0

Printed and manufactured in China
Written by Jenny Cox
Illustrated by Rachel Baines

Bedtime Stories
for Girls

igloobooks

Contents

Ballet Magic

Amelia wished that she could prove to her mum how much she wanted ballet lessons. She wished so hard that, one day, a mysterious parcel arrived for her in the post. Amelia ripped it open to find a pair of tattered, old ballet shoes.

"Who would send horrible, old ballet shoes?" thought Amelia. Suddenly, a cloud of sparkly, pink dust fizzed around her feet. Amelia looked down in amazement. The tatty slippers looked like they were brand new.

POOF! Suddenly, Amelia found herself in a magical wood, wearing a beautiful tutu. "Hello," said a voice. It was a ballerina fairy. "I'll help you to show your mum how well you can dance," said the fairy.

The fairy showed Amelia how to stretch, pirouette and leap.
All afternoon, they danced on an enchanted stage. Soon, Amelia
was dancing like a real prima ballerina.

More fairies fluttered nearby and lifted Amelia high into the air as she danced and twirled. "It's time to go home now," said the ballerina fairy. "Goodbye fairies," said Amelia, "thank you for helping me."

POOF! Suddenly, Amelia was back home. She ran to show Mum her new moves. "I'm impressed," said Mum. "You can have ballet lessons." Amelia's dream had come true and it was all thanks to a little magic.

The Tooth Fairy's Visit

Chloe's tooth had been wobbling for ages. One day, as she was jumping in and out of the fairy ring at the bottom of the garden, the tooth fell out. "Yes!" cried Chloe. "I've lost my first tooth at last." Chloe ran inside to show her mum.

"Put your tooth in here," said Mum, handing
Chloe a sparkly pouch. "In the night, the
Tooth Fairy will come and wave her magic
wand over the bag and leave a special surprise."

13

That night, Chloe slipped the pouch under her pillow and fell asleep. As the clock struck midnight, she heard a tinkling noise. Right in front of her was a real fairy.

14

"I'm the Tooth Fairy," she said, waving her wand and taking the special pouch. There was a shower of sparkles. Suddenly, Chloe was in the garden and surrounded by fairies!

One fairy with golden hair took Chloe by the hand and danced in the fairy ring with her, as the other fairies sang in sweet voices. Chloe giggled as she danced round in circles.

The fairies flew about busily and Chloe looked up
to see them making a magical feast. There were yummy
cakes, delicious cookies and lots of treats.

16

Chloe and the fairies had so much
fun eating the enchanted fairy food.

17

Soon, Chloe was so full that she began to feel sleepy.
"It's time to go back to bed," said the Tooth Fairy.

Back in Chloe's bedroom,
the fairy smiled and pinged
her wand over the pouch.
Chloe thanked the Tooth Fairy
and snuggled down to sleep.

The next morning, Chloe woke up and reached under her pillow for the pouch. The tooth had gone! In its place was a golden coin.

Chloe rushed downstairs to show her mum. "I told you there would be a magical surprise," said Mum. "Next time one of your teeth falls out, you'll know exactly what to do."

Chloe gave her mum a big hug. "Thanks, Mum," she said. "You're the best."

Princess for a Day

If I were a princess for a day,
I'd wake up and shout, "Yippee! Hurray!"
I would slip on my prettiest gown,
And top it off with a sparkly crown.

Outside my window I would hear a, "Neigh!"
And decide to ride my pony all day.
I'd feed him lovely, sweet sugar lumps.
We'd gallop around, leaping over jumps.

I'd ask my friends to come for high tea,
And sit underneath the apple tree.
We'd eat cakes, crisps and sandwiches, too.
We'd chat just like real princesses do.

At night, there would be a royal ball.
I'd wear my fanciest dress of all.
I'd sing and dance and laugh and play,
If only I were a princess for a day.

23

Rainy Day Farm

It was Saturday morning and Keira was really excited because Dad was taking her to a farm. When Keira pulled back her bedroom curtains, however, she saw that it was raining outside. "It's so wet!" she cried.

When Keira and Dad arrived at the farm, the rain had made big, muddy puddles everywhere. Suddenly, a flock of sheep came rushing by. SPLOSH!
They splashed water everywhere.

"Never mind," chuckled Dad.
"Let's go and see the piglets."

Keira cooed over the piglets, with their cute, curly tails. Just then, the mummy pig flopped down into the mud with a grunt. SPLAT! Keira and Dad were splattered with mud!

Next, Keira and Dad visited the hen house.
As they opened the creaky door, the chickens
flew out and their feathers flitted everywhere.

Dad and Keira looked at one another
and giggled. "I think it's time we had
some lunch," said Dad.

The rain had stopped, so Dad and Keira sat at a picnic table and got out their sandwiches and drinks. While Keira was opening her bottle of fizzy lemonade, a cheeky goat snuck up and greedily gobbled up her sandwiches.

"Oh, dear," said Farmer Bill. "I think you had better come on inside."

He took Keira and Dad inside and gave them a hot drink and cookies. Keira cuddled one of the fluffy farm kittens and smiled.

"Thanks, Farmer Bill," said Keira. "Thanks, Dad."
"This has been the most eventful farm visit ever!"

Mermaid Friends

Megan was very excited. Her friends were coming over to have a mermaid party in the garden. Megan went outside to fill the paddling pool with water when she felt a spot of rain on her cheek.

"Mummy, it's raining outside!" cried Megan. She looked at her special mermaid outfit and began to cry. "Don't worry," said Mum, coming to see what all the fuss was about. "You can still play your game. I'll help you to set it up in the living room instead."

Mum went upstairs and brought down a patterned blanket and some sea-green scarves. She put them on the sofa, then pinned on pictures of starfish and coral fish. "It's a coral reef!" said Megan, smiling.

Next, Mum decorated the sideboard with her collection of crystals.
In the middle, she placed a glitter lamp and arranged sparkly hair clips,
hairbrushes and mirrors all around it. The lamp lit up the room and
created silvery shadows, just like water ripples.

"What about the rock pool?" asked Megan.
Mum suggested they use Megan's old baby bath.
She filled it up with water, then dropped
in plastic fish, sponges and purple
bath salts. It was perfect!

Megan changed into her special mermaid outfit. As she twirled in front of the mirror, the glistening mermaid dress shimmered and twinkled.

Just then, the doorbell rang. Ding-dong! "Hello Suzy, hello Bella and Pip," said Megan. "Welcome to my mermaid party!"

Megan and her friends had so much fun playing in their enchanted, magical mermaid world. Megan and Suzy gently splashed in the rock pool, while Bella and Pip chatted on the coral reef and sang mermaid songs.

Mum came into the room with lots of yummy treats for the girls. "I'm really glad it rained," said Megan, smiling and all her friends agreed.

37

Lucy's Birthday Surprise

It was Lucy's birthday and she was downstairs, opening her presents.
"Happy Birthday!" said Mum and Dad, smiling. "We've got a big
surprise for you today. You're going to love it." Lucy was very excited.
She couldn't wait to find out what the surprise would be.

After a yummy breakfast, Mum took Lucy shopping to buy a new dress. "Choose whatever you like," said Mum. Lucy flicked through the rails and decided on a pink dress with a lovely, frilly skirt.

"Is this the surprise?" asked Lucy.
"No," replied Mum, with a secret smile.
"Let's go to Gran's house and see if your surprise is there."

At Gran's house, in the garden,
they had a drink and some cupcakes.
Gran gave Lucy a gift box and
inside was a sparkly tiara.

"Wow," said Lucy, "is this my special surprise?"
"No!" cried Mum and Gran, giggling together.

40

Back home, Lucy put on her new dress and tiara to show Dad. She looked at herself in the hall mirror. "I'm ready!" she cried, but there was no reply. Where was everyone?

Suddenly, Lucy heard a noise upstairs. She ran up and opened her bedroom door.

"SURPRISE!" cried Mum, Dad and Gran. Lucy's room had
been transformed into a princess palace, with a beautiful bed,
and a throne by her window! "Wow!" said Lucy, gasping.
"This is amazing!"

42

"Dad did all of this when we were out, so we could keep it a secret," said Mum, holding a cake with candles on. Everyone sang 'Happy Birthday' and Lucy felt very happy. Her birthday surprise was definitely worth waiting for.

Party Pyjamas

Suzy had been invited to her first ever pyjama party and was looking for her best pink pyjamas. She searched around in her drawer and finally found them. "Oh, no!" Suzy cried. There was a massive hole in the trouser leg!

Suzy was worried she wouldn't be able to go to the party.

"Let's take you shopping for new pyjamas," said Mum.

"We'll have to be quick, because the party starts soon and you don't want to miss it."

Mum took Suzy to a shop where they sold lots of pyjamas.
The shop assistant brought different pairs for Suzy to try on.

There were big ones...

... and small ones.

There were spotty ones...

... and stripy ones.

Mum even found monster pyjamas and rocket pyjamas, but Suzy didn't like any of them. She looked at her reflection in the mirror and pulled a face. "I look silly," she said with a sob. "Now I won't be able to go to the party."

Just then, the sales assistant came over.
She held up a cute kitten sleepsuit.
"How about this?" she said, smiling.
"It's perfect!" cried Suzy.

Suzy tried the sleepsuit on. It was
as if it was made especially for her.
She kept it on while Mum paid.

When Suzy arrived at the party her friends gathered round her.
"We LOVE your sleepsuit!" they cried. Suzy felt really happy.
She had a brilliant time at the party. Having a hole in her
pyjamas had been a good thing after all!

The Missing Crown

There was a terrible commotion in the palace one morning.
The king had lost his crown and everyone was looking for it.
Princess Emma and her puppy, Charlie, were looking, too.

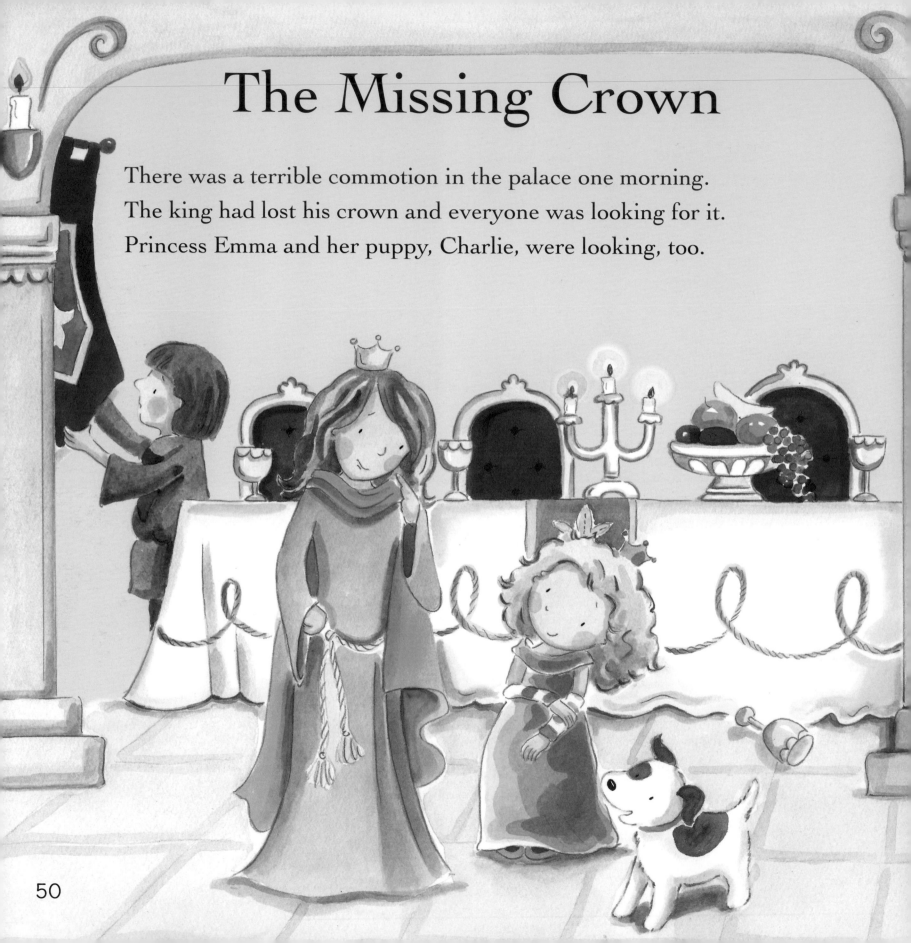

"Please make sure Charlie is kept on his lead," said the queen.
"You know what a naughty puppy he can be."
"Yes, Mum," groaned Princess Emma.

51

Emma gave Charlie a big cuddle. She tried to tie on his lead, but he saw the king's cat, Ginger and dashed off. Barking, he ran across the lawn after her. "Charlie!" Emma shouted, chasing after the runaway puppy.

Charlie chased Ginger through the palace gardens. Emma tried to catch him, but he was too fast. She watched as Charlie raced after Ginger and ended up running right through the muddy vegetable patch.

Charlie ran through the rose garden and stopped by the royal washing lines. Emma looked in horror as he shook his muddy, wet coat all over the freshly washed tablecloths.

Emma chased Charlie as he raced back into the palace, to the kitchen. Sniffing the ground, Charlie found some cookies cooling on the table. He chomped them all up before the cook, or Emma, could stop him.

Charlie thought it was all a big game.
When Emma finally caught up with him,
he was sitting on the king's throne.

"Come here, naughty," she said.
Emma felt something heavy behind the
royal cushion. It was her father's crown!

"Well, I never!" cried the king, coming into the room. "Charlie found my crown. What a clever puppy."

After that, no one ever thought Charlie was a nuisance again.

57

My Brother Josh

My brother Josh is a bit of a pain,
He wakes up at night again and again.
During the day he makes lots of loud noise,
He runs away with all my best toys.

My brother Josh makes lots and lots of mess.
He gets mud and paint on my special dress.
Mum gives him a bath to make him all clean,
Then puts my dress in the washing machine.

My brother Josh doesn't like to eat food,
He flicks and plays with it, just to be rude.
He spills his water all over the floor,
Then throws his ice cream at the kitchen door.

Josh is a handful, that is plain to see,
But something happens when he smiles at me.
Josh is so special, he's like no other.
I'm really glad that Josh is my brother.

Rainbow Party

It was the night before Sophie's birthday. She sat in bed with her cute kitten, Caramel, planning the theme of her party. Sophie was determined that everything had to be pink.

Sophie loved pink. She had pastel pink teddies nestled on her bed, bright pink pyjamas and a wardrobe full of pink clothes.

"You could have other shades too, Sophie," said Mum.
"I want my party to be pink," said Sophie, "I wish the whole world was pink." Sophie giggled and snuggled down to sleep.

Suddenly, Sophie woke up. She blinked and looked around. Everything
was pink. She tiptoed to the bathroom and looked in the mirror.
Her hair and skin were the shade of bubblegum. "Cool," said Sophie.

Next, Sophie crept downstairs to the
kitchen and opened the fridge door.
Sure enough, all the food inside
was pink.

"These look yummy," she said,
eating what looked like pink sweets.
"Yuck!" cried Sophie. The sweets
were Brussels sprouts!

Just then, Sophie heard Caramel meowing outside the door. She opened it and shrieked. There were kittens everywhere and they were all pink! "Which one is Caramel?" cried Sophie.

Suddenly, Sophie woke up. Her room was back to normal and so was her kitten, Caramel. She had been dreaming! "What a relief," said Sophie, running downstairs to see her mum.

Sophie didn't want a pink party after all. "I want a rainbow theme," she said to her mum and Mum thought this was a very good idea.

"We'll make you a wonderful rainbow party,"
said Mum and that is exactly what they did.
Sophie had a brilliant time and she had to agree that
a rainbow was better than just pink any day!

69

Dress-up Day

One day, Daisy and Jade wished so hard to have a dress-up adventure that their wish came true. A whirl of glitter whooshed into their bedroom and swirled all around, leaving behind a sparkly box on the ground.

Inside the bright box were magical, enchanted wands, sparkly dressing-up outfits, necklaces and rings. Daisy and Jade tried on two enchanted ballgowns. POOF! Suddenly, they were in a magical world.

Daisy and Jade danced as princesses and wore glittery jewels.

They became mystical mermaids, diving in pools.

Then they fluttered through the sky above gardens and ponds.

POOF! Suddenly, Daisy and Jade were back home.
It had been a brilliant adventure and now they were ready for bed.
They couldn't wait to make another magical wish tomorrow!

73

Poppy's Surprise

Poppy was staying the night with her Gran. She was worried about being bored, but Mum had told her that she might be in for a surprise. "Is there anything to do?" she asked Gran, in the kitchen.

"Why don't you pop up to the attic room?" replied Gran, smiling.

"There are lots of interesting things to look at in there."

Poppy didn't think there would be many surprises in a dusty, old attic.

75

In the attic, there were piles of old things. In a dusty chest, Poppy found a tutu and ballet slippers. There was something else in the chest, too.

Poppy found a pretty music box, with a ballerina on top. Poppy wound the key and it played a lovely tune.

The ballerina twirled and something amazing happened.
The room began to change. Magic sparkles twinkled in a whirl.
Suddenly, everything became bright and shiny. Then, in a flash of light,
the ballerina came to life.

"Wow!" cried Poppy, staring at the beautiful ballerina. "Hello, Poppy," said the ballerina. "Will you dance with me?" she asked.

Poppy nodded excitedly. She put on the tutu and ballet slippers. Then, the ballerina took her hand and they twirled to the music.

The ballerina showed Poppy how to move like a real dancer. Poppy giggled as she followed the ballerina out of the attic and down the stairs.

They twirled past the lounge where Gran was having a nap. "This is such fun!" said Poppy.

Poppy and the ballerina danced together beautifully, all afternoon. Then, it was time for the ballerina to go. Poppy turned the little music box key gently. "Goodbye, see you soon," said the ballerina. In a flash, she turned back into a figurine.

Everything was just as it had been. Poppy ran downstairs to tell Gran. "You were right, Gran," she said. "The attic is magic." Gran handed Poppy a piece of cake. "I know," she said with a smile and they both burst out laughing.

Magical Misty

Florence lived next door to a pony sanctuary. Each day, she helped Sally, the owner, care for the ponies that were too old to ride. Florence loved them all, but she wished she had a special pony of her own.

Then one day, Misty, a little pony arrived. "She's very shy, but very special," said Sally. At first, Misty hid away when Florence came to visit the stable. Florence talked gently and gave her a carrot and Misty munched it, happily. "She likes you," said Sally.

Each day, Florence came to visit Misty. She talked to her and walked her round the paddock. Then, late one afternoon, when Misty was in the meadow, she let Florence sit on her back. Misty began to trot and then she began to canter.

Florence looked down and saw that Misty had two beautiful wings.
"Wow!" cried Florence as Misty swooped into the sky and began to fly.
Some little birds flew by, tweeting loudly. "Hello," called Florence.

Misty lifted Florence higher into the sky, over lakes and hills.
Florence spotted a rainbow and Misty flew over it and back under it.
Florence wanted to fly all day, but soon it was time to go back home.

"Sally!" called Florence, as they landed with a soft thud. "Misty can fly!"
"I told you she was special," said Sally, smiling. "Now you can have your
very own pony to ride and it will be our little secret."

Time for Bed

It was late in the day, the sun had nearly set.
Bea said to her mum, "I don't feel that tired yet."
Mum said that soon she would be a big sleepy head,
Just like the animals that were going to bed.

They saw cute bunnies going hoppity, hop, hop,
Into their burrows with a floppity, flop, flop.
Tired baby squirrels scampered into the trees.
Pretty butterflies fluttered on the evening breeze.

Tiny birds chirruped and flew home to their cosy nest.
Tweet-tweet, tweet-tweet they sang, all ready for a rest.
Hamster was snuggled down and so was Puppy, too.
"Come on, Bea," said Mum. "Now it is bedtime for you."

The sun had gone down and the day was at an end.
Bea had said goodnight to each of her animal friends.
She jumped into her bed and snuggled up tight.
Mum kissed her and whispered, "Goodnight."

Night Light

After a long day unpacking in their new cottage, it was Alice's bedtime. "Night-night," said Mum turning out the light. This bedroom was much darker than Alice's old one and she felt a bit scared.

Alice opened the curtains to let moonlight shine in. It lit up the room,
but then a big cloud covered the moon up. So, Alice found her pink torch.
It made strange shadows and shapes that frightened her.

Alice remembered her glow-in-the-dark fairy stickers.
They looked very pretty, but they didn't give off much light.
Suddenly, one dropped off the wall and made Alice jump.
"Mum, I'm scared!" she cried out.

Mum gave Alice a lovely cuddle. "I used to be frightened of the dark, too," she said, "but there was something that always made me feel better."

Mum went off and rustled around in one of the packing boxes.

"It's my old night light," Mum told Alice, switching it on. The night light glowed and had a picture of a fairy dancing in front of the moon, waving her wand as she flew. "I love it!" cried Alice and she knew, at last, she would have a very good night's sleep.